Level 3

Ham and Cheese

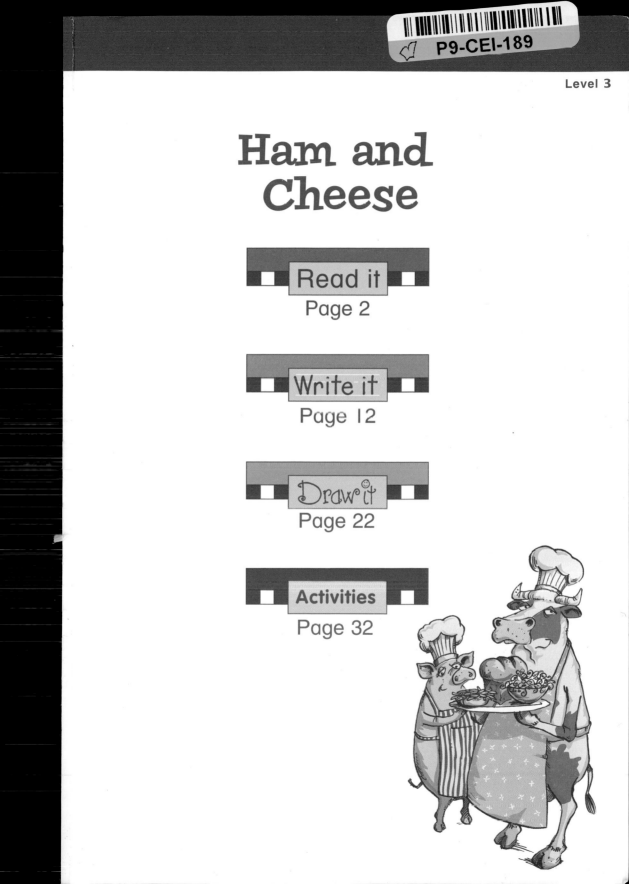

Ham and Cheese lived on a farm. They used to work hard all day.

At first glance, they looked like just a pig and a cow—but Ham and Cheese had a big secret.

Every night when the farmer and his
wife were fast asleep, Ham and Cheese
would tiptoe into the kitchen . . .

. . . and cook three yummy meals for the next day.

Ham cooked breakfast. He made fresh apple pancakes, corn muffins, and orange juice.

Cheese cooked lunch. She made
tomato soup, hot pepper sandwiches,
and french fries.

For dinner, Ham and Cheese worked
together. They baked bread, cooked
noodles, and made green beans.

Read it

Then, every morning, when the farmer and his wife woke up, they would look into the kitchen and see the big feast!

They did not know where it came from,
but the taste of it made them happy
and sleepy all day.

And of course that made Ham and Cheese and all the other animals happy too!

Look at the picture on each page, and then write the story in your own words.

Ham and Cheese lived on a farm. They used to work hard all day.

At first glance, they looked like just a pig and a cow—but Ham and Cheese had a big secret.

Every night when the farmer and his
wife were fast asleep, Ham and Cheese
would tiptoe into the kitchen . . .

Draw it

. . . and cook three yummy meals for the next day.

Ham cooked breakfast. He made fresh apple pancakes, corn muffins, and orange juice.

Draw it

Cheese cooked lunch. She made
tomato soup, hot pepper sandwiches,
and french fries.

For dinner, Ham and Cheese worked together. They baked bread, cooked noodles, and made green beans.

Draw it

Then, every morning, when the farmer and his wife woke up, they would look into the kitchen and see the big feast!

They did not know where it came from,
but the taste of it made them happy
and sleepy all day.

Draw it

And of course that made Ham and Cheese and all the other animals happy too!

Activities

Read it

Make fact books! Have your child or student select a nonfiction book. Then, read the book aloud to the child. Ask the child to recall as many facts as possible from the book. As the child recalls the facts, write down his or her words. Put those facts into simple sentences, and staple them together into a mini book. Title the book "My Facts About _____." This will be a great book for your child or student to read back to you and a great way to help him or her learn important facts.

Write it

Experiment with alliteration! Introduce your child or student to the concept of alliteration, the repetition of the same initial consonant sound in two or more words in a line of writing. Model an example of alliteration by writing a sentence such as "Monkeys make millions of marshmallows." Now challenge your child or student to write his or her own sentence using alliteration. If the child is really adventurous, he or she can make a book of alliteration with a sentence for each letter of the alphabet!

Draw it

Create a travel poster! After reading a book, have your child or student make a travel poster inviting tourists to visit the setting of the story. For instance, if the story about life on the Moon, the child can draw a picture of the Moon with the slogan, "Come visit the Moon!" All he or she will need is a large piece of paper or poster board and crayons. Before beginning the poster, have the child describe the setting as in much detail as possible. Then, let the child's imagination soar as he or she re-creates the setting in his or her own artistic style.

A NOTE TO PARENTS:
When children create their own spellings for words they don't know, they are using **inventive spelling**. For the beginner, the act of writing is more important than the correctness of form. Sounding out words and predicting how they will be spelled reinforces an understanding of the connection between letters and sounds. Eventually, through experimenting with spelling patterns and repeated exposure to standard spelling, children will learn and use the correct form in their own writing. Until then, inventive spelling encourages early experimentation and self-expression in writing and nurtures a child's confidence as a writer.